Let fear disappear,

is here!

Giant killer socks are on the loose in
Trashland . . . and they stink!

It's time to fight crime with slime!

Collect all the cool cards and check out
the special website for more slimy stuff:

www.slimesquad.co.uk

D0320995

Don't miss the rest of the series:

THE SLIME SQUAD vs THE FEARSOME FISTS
THE SLIME SQUAD vs THE TOXIC TEETH
THE SLIME SQUAD vs THE CYBER-POOS
THE SLIME SQUAD vs THE SUPERNATURAL SQUID
THE SLIME SQUAD vs THE LAST-CHANCE CHICKEN

Also available by the same author,
these fantastic series:

COWS IN ACTION

ASTROSAURS

ASTROSAURS ACADEMY

www.stevecolebooks.co.uk

THE SLIME SQUAD

VS

THE KILLER SOCKS

by Steve Cole

Illustrated by Woody Fox

RED FOX

THE SLIME SQUAD vs THE KILLER SOCKS
A RED FOX BOOK 978 1 862 30880 0

Published in Great Britain by Red Fox Books,
an imprint of Random House Children's Books
A Random House Group Company

This edition published 2011

1 3 5 7 9 10 8 6 4 2

Copyright © Steve Cole, 2011
Cover illustration and cards © Andy Parker, 2011
Map © Steve Cole and Dynamo Design, 2011
Illustrations copyright © Woody Fox, 2011

The right of Steve Cole to be identified as the author of this work
has been asserted in accordance with the Copyright, Designs and
Patents Act 1988.

The Random House Group Limited supports the Forest Stewardship
Council (FSC), the leading international forest certification
organization. All our titles that are printed on Greenpeace-approved
FSC-certified paper carry the FSC logo. Our paper procurement policy
can be found at www.rbooks.co.uk/environment.

Mixed Sources
Product group from well-managed
forests and other controlled sources
www.fsc.org Cert no. TT-COC-2139
© 1996 Forest Stewardship Council
FSC

Red Fox Books are published by Random House Children's Books,
61–63 Uxbridge Road, London W5 5SA

www.kidsatrandomhouse.co.uk
www.rbooks.co.uk

Addresses for companies within The Random House Group Limited can
be found at: www.randomhouse.co.uk/offices.htm

THE RANDOM HOUSE GROUP Limited Reg. No. 954009

A CIP catalogue record for this book is available from
the British Library.

Printed in the UK by CPI Bookmaque, Croydon

For Helen and James Grice

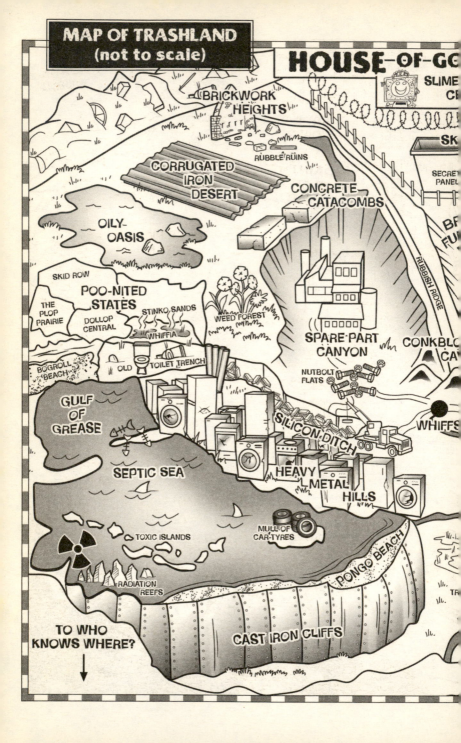

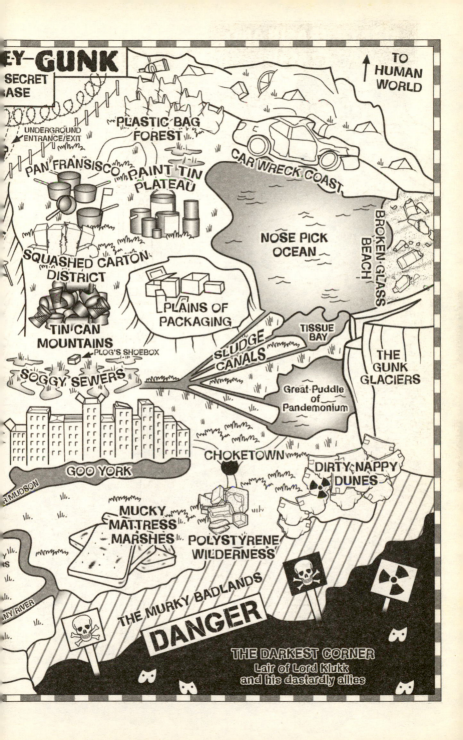

ONCE UPON A SLIME...

The old rubbish dump was far from anywhere. An enormous, mucky, rusty landscape of thousands of thrown-away things.

It had been closed for years. Abandoned. Forgotten.

And then Godfrey Gunk came along.

Godfrey wasn't just a mad scientist. He was a SUPER-BONKERS scientist! And he was very worried about the amount of pollution and rubbish in the world. His dream was to create marvellous mutant mini-monsters out of chemical goo – monsters who would clean up the planet by eating, drinking and generally devouring all types of trash. So Godfrey bought the old rubbish dump as the perfect testing-ground and got to work.

Of course, he wanted to make good, friendly, peaceful monsters, so he was careful to keep the nastiest, most toxic chemicals separate from the rest. He worked for years and years . . .

And got nowhere.

In the end, penniless and miserable, Godfrey wrecked his lab, scattered his experiments all over the dump, and moved away, never to return.

But what Godfrey didn't know was that long ago, tons of radioactive sludge had been accidentally dumped here. And soon, its potent powers kick-started the monster chemistry the mad scientist had tried so hard to create!

Life began to form. Amazing mini-monsters sprang up with incredible speed.

Bold, inventive monsters, who made a wonderful, whiffy world for themselves from the rubbish around them – a world they named Trashland.

For many years, they lived and grew in peace. But then the radiation reached a lead-lined box in the darkest corner of the rubbish dump – the place where Godfrey had chucked the most toxic, dangerous gunk of all.

Slowly, very slowly, monsters began to grow here too.

Different monsters.

Evil monsters that now threaten the whole of Trashland.

Only one force for good stands against them. A small band of slightly sticky superheroes . . .

The Slime Squad!

Chapter One
A SINISTER "SOMETHING"

Night had fallen over Trashland like a giant's shadow. The moon was lost behind clouds, and yet the skies over the town of Whiffsville held an eerie, flickering glow . . .

A big factory was on fire!

Flames licked at the darkness. The streets around were all but lost in a thick cloud of smoke.

Monster workers, their blue skin blackened with soot, staggered out of the factory, coughing and choking.

"Help!" one monster yelled at the top of her lungs. "My friends are trapped inside . . . Can't anybody help us?"

"They certainly can," came a froggy voice from out of the darkness. "Let fear disappear – the Slime Squad is here!" With a rattle of metal pants, a pale yellow frog-monster in a crash helmet landed beside her. "Furp LeBurp, at your service, madam."

"I'm Jurley, the factory boss," said the monster. "My team and I were working the night shift when this fire started up out of nowhere."

"Don't worry." Furp leaped onto the side of the smouldering building and started scaling the wall with his slimy hands and feet. "The super-scanner in my helmet will soon show me exactly where your friends are stuck."

"And then what?" Jurley fretted.

"And then WE will save them," came a booming voice.

Jurley jumped as a large, crimson crab-monster in golden shorts came striding up on three stocky legs. "You . . . you're Danjo Jigg. The Slime Squad really *is* here!"

"In the ever-loving, baddie-shoving flesh," Danjo agreed, snapping his powerful pincers. "Sorry for the hold-up – we've just been clearing everyone away from the area."

3

"Right!" A sharp-snouted she-monster in a golden leotard swung into sight on the end of a sticky slime-rope and landed beside Danjo. "If we don't get this fire under control fast, the whole of Whiffsville could go up in smoke."

"Zill Billie!" Jurley stared — one part poodle and two parts atomic skunk, the Slime Squad's third member was instantly recognizable. "But . . . what if you *can't* stop the flames? It's the fourth fire at one of my fabric factories in as many days."

"We'll sort everything out," Danjo assured her. "Even now, our leader is inspecting the whole building, checking out the blaze from all angles, staying cool and calm while he plans our next move—"

"*Arrrrrrrrrgh!*" A burly, orangey bear-rat monster in heavy iron boots came hurtling out of the blazing factory, trailing smoke behind him as he ran in frantic circles. "My tail's on fire! My tail's on fire! Arrrrrgh!"

"This is Plog." Danjo grinned at Jurley. "As leaders go, he's *smokin'* hot!"

Zill stuck out one of her six legs and tripped up Plog.

"Oof!"

Then Danjo raised his right pincer and scooshed icy slime over Plog's behind, putting out the fire.

"Ahhhhhhhhh," sighed Plog, his bottom gently steaming. He wore a threadbare waistcoat and trousers,

 and a mask made from Danjo's old shorts. He looked up at Jurley and smiled. "You'd better get to safety. Tackling this blaze is a job for the Slime Squad."

"I thought your job was fighting evil monsters!" said Jurley.

Plog nodded thoughtfully. It was hard to believe that, up until a few months ago, evil monsters had been unheard of in Trashland. In those days, the Slime Squad had gentler duties like rescuing trapped insects or sorting out traffic jams. But then an evil mutant chicken-thing called Lord Klukk had turned up with a horde of toxic, terrifying allies, determined to take over Trashland – and the Slime Squad's new mission was to stop these baddies at any cost!

"There are definitely monsters still stuck inside this building," Furp reported from the smouldering wall. "My scanner is showing their precise location . . . But how can we help them?"

"The fire is blocking all ways in and out at ground level," said Plog ruefully, clutching his tail. "Furp, what state is the roof in?"

Furp climbed right to the top of the building and peered through the smoke. "There's a massive hole in its middle. It's completely burned away."

"Perfect!" Plog declared. "Zill, get up there. Quickly!"

Zill spat a slime-line all the way to the top of the wall and swiftly scaled it. Plog and Danjo climbed after her, their arms and legs aching, their lungs prickling with every smoky breath.

The flames were rising up from the giant cardboard construction. Plog thought about the workers stuck inside and forced himself to climb faster.

As they scrambled onto the roof, Plog turned to Zill. "Spit a slime-strand at Furp!" he urged her.

"Why, what have I done?" Furp protested. But Zill did as she was told, sending a slightly smoky slime-strand clear across the hole in the roof. It stuck securely to the other side.

"There! An instant tightrope." Plog turned to Danjo. "I only hope that *you* are a good tightrope walker!"

Danjo boggled. "You want me to step out and balance over that enormous hole?"

"Yep. And then I want you to squirt as much icy slime in the air as you can," Plog told him. "Hopefully that slimy sprinkler will put out the fire!"

"But that'll take time,' Zill realized. "What do we do about the poor monsters trapped down there?"

"Furp will show us where they are," said Plog. "If you and I attach ourselves to two of your stickiest, stretchiest slime-lines, we can bungee jump down into the factory, grab them—"

"And bounce straight back out again with the workers safely in our arms!" Zill beamed. "Smart thinking, Fur-boy. Let's do it!"

Danjo was already balanced precariously in the middle of the slimy tightrope, spraying blue slime in an icy shower. The flames below hissed and sizzled in the downpour.

Zill spun two long slime-lines for Plog and herself, and secured one end of each to the roof. Plog tied the other end of his slimy bungee cord around his waist while Zill did the same with hers.

Checking his scanner, Furp steered
Zill into a particular position at the
edge of the hole. "There should be two

workers directly beneath
you here . . ."

"Not for long!" Zill
leaped through the
hole in the roof, falling
down into the smoky
blackness.

"Geronimoooo-onster!"
A few seconds later, her bungee cord
catapulted her straight up and out again
with her poodly legs wrapped around a
stunned, sooty blue character.

"Yessss!" Furp jumped
and caught them both
in midair, delivering
them safely to the
side of the hole with
a CLOMP and a
clatter. "Rescue stage
one complete!"

"I'm Noodle," said
the worker weakly.
"Please, save my
friend Horace.
Some shelves fell on
him. I've been
trying to dig him
out."

"On my way,"
Zill cried. She
jumped down again,
reappearing moments later with Horace
in her grasp, collapsing on the scorched
cardboard ledge. "There!"

"Yahoo!" Wobbling wildly on the
tightrope, still pumping out ice-slime,
Danjo beamed at them through the
smoke. "Way to go, guys!"

Plog gave Zill a thumbs-up. "And
now it's my turn . . ."

Furp nodded. "If you take two steps to
your left, my dear Plog, you should find a
rather bigger worker waiting for rescue."

"Er . . . I don't think there's anyone else inside," said Noodle, still tangled up in Zill's paws. "All the other workers got out in time."

"My scanner says differently," Furp assured him.

"I'll drop in and find out for sure," said Plog. "Here goes . . ."

Taking a deep breath, he jumped down into the hot, smoky darkness. Danjo's sprinkler was taking effect, but the flames were still frighteningly fierce. The slime-line round Plog tautened and stretched, slowing his fall. He reached out blindly to grab another blue factory worker . . .

But his arms closed on something very different. Something huge and lumpy and woollen. Something cold and horrid to the touch. Plog's nose twitched as a whiff of mouldy cheese and cabbage and wet, sweaty armpits filled the air.

The sinister *something* wriggled and writhed in his grip. "Hey, I'm only trying to help!" Plog protested. He caught a glimpse of red skin in the flickering firelight – then gasped as his slimy bungee cord snapped and the 'something' slammed him to the ground.

With a rattling roar, the creature reared up over Plog, round gaping mouth stretched wide, ready to gobble him up . . .

Chapter Two

THE FABRIC THIEVES

"Who are you?" Plog demanded as the shadowy monster loomed ever closer. "What are you doing inside a burning factory?"

Hissing and gurgling, the shadowy creature's only answer was to spit a jet of flame from his wide open mouth! Plog barely rolled clear in time.

"Hey!" he shouted. "Did you *start* this fire?"

The monster nodded his misshapen head and laughed nastily.

But then a loud cry sounded – "Whoooaaaaa!" – and something large and crimson crashed down on top of Plog's attacker. "Oof! I fell off the tightrope. Good job my butt found a cushion . . ."

"Danjo!" Plog cried. "That is no 'cushion' – he breathes fire. He's alive!"

Danjo jumped up and scrambled away. "Alive?"

Suddenly, there was a series of strange noises: *STR-EE-EE-TCH! Boing! WHOOOOOOSH!*

Plog's ears pricked up. "What was that rush of wind?"

Danjo gave him a look. "Whoever smelled it, dealt it."

"Not that sort of wind," Plog told him. "It sounded like a rocket taking off . . ."

"I'll just put out these fires," said Danjo, "then we'll have a proper look."

But as the cool crab-creature buried the last of the blaze beneath a pile of slimy slush, it was clear that the fire-breathing 'something' had gone. The factory was empty.

The next moment, Zill and Furp came scooting down a slime-line with Noodle and Horace – the blue workers – on their backs.

"Danjo, are you and Plog all right?" Zill asked worriedly.

"My scanner showed that the other living thing down here just vanished," Furp added.

"It certainly seems to have disappeared," said Plog. Quickly he explained all that had happened.

"I'm not surprised this weird monster took off when Danjo fell on him," said Zill. "But how come we didn't see him leave?"

Furp shook his head, puzzled. "And why did he start a fire here in the first place?"

"Maybe those other factory fires were started on purpose too," said Danjo.

"Let's look for clues," Plog suggested. "The other factories burned to the ground, but thanks to Danjo's ice-goo this one's still standing."

Horace nodded to a closed door nearby. "It looks like the main storeroom has hardly been touched at all."

Just then, Jurley came puffing in from outside. "Horace! Noodle! I'm so glad you're safe."

"Thanks to the Slime Squad," Noodle said happily, pulling open the storeroom door. "And look, that massive pile of fabric you put in here this evening should be completely—"

19

"Gone!" squeaked Jurley, staring inside. "Oh, no! All my poshest material, in so many beautiful colours — it must have gone up in smoke."

Furp hopped inside. "Nothing has burned in here — there's no ash at all."

Plog nodded slowly. "Then — that fire-breathing thing must have stolen the fabrics . . . But why?"

Dirty and sore, the Squaddies drove back home to their secret base in the Slime-mobile, their invisible mega-monster truck. As day began to break, Zill steered them into the secret passage that led to the underground garage.

"Poor old Jurley," she said. "All four of her factories, burned down and burgled!"

Plog nodded. "I wonder where that smelly, lumpy fire-starter will strike next?"

"The All-Seeing PIE will know what to do," Danjo declared.

Zill parked the Slime-mobile, and everyone ran to PIE's office. Plog hoped Danjo was right. PIE – short for Perfect Intelligent  Electronics – was the Squad's computerized boss. His clever, all-seeing sensors were scattered wide and far throughout Trashland; whenever monsters were in trouble, he sent the Squad off to sort things out.

Danjo and Zill heaved open the office door to reveal a massive, battered computer with a funny face on his screen – PIE in all his high-tech glory.

"PIE," Plog called. "Did you see that fire-starting fabric thief coming or going?"

"ARE YOU BEING CHEEKY?" boomed a mechanical voice suspiciously.

"Er, no," said Plog, gulping. "Just puzzled."

"My sensors detected *something* leaving the fabric factory in Whiffsville at incredible speed tonight," PIE confirmed. "Possibly some sort of rocket . . ."

Furp nodded thoughtfully. "That would explain how the thief took all that material with him."

"Do rockets go 'boing'?" wondered Danjo. "That's the sound we heard."

"I am checking my recordings of the other factory fires for things that go 'boing'," PIE assured him. "I will study the evidence frame by frame! Pixel by pixel! Nano-byte by banana!"

Plog frowned. "Nano-byte by banana?"

"Whoops, sorry, I got muddled with my shopping list," said PIE. "Buy a banana. They're good for you."

"This whole thing is bananas," Zill sighed. "Why would anyone who wanted to steal a mountain of material set fire to the place as well?"

"So no one would know they had taken it?" PIE suggested.

"Do you think Lord Klukk is behind this?" asked Plog nervously.

Danjo frowned. "What would he want with a load of posh material?"

"That clucking fiend is always plotting mayhem from the shadows," PIE grumbled. "And he has many dangerous friends. We must be on our guard." Suddenly exclamation marks appeared all over his scuffed screen. "Warning!" he boomed. "A fire has started at the Cotton-Picking Thread Store in Goo  York, just outside Monstahattan. It could mean the start of another robbery. SHIFT!"

★

Within seconds, Plog, Zill, Furp and Danjo were back in the Slime-mobile.

"Hang on, guys!" Zill shouted, leaping into the driver's seat and revving the engines. "I'm putting the pedal to the metal – NOW!"

The Slime-mobile surged forward and roared away, leaving big stripes of burnt invisible rubber in its wake. Plog held onto his seat for dear life as the journey grew faster and wilder – it felt as though Zill had put the pedal right *through* the metal and then tied it to the back of a rocket-powered super-elephant!

"I LOVE Goo York," said the she-
monster dreamily. "It's full of fab clothes!
All the top monster fashion designers
live there. In fact, I haven't driven this
fast since the Goo York
January sales!"

Plog pointed through
the windscreen. "That
must be the place. Look!"

The scene ahead was
lit yellow in the Slime-
mobile's headlights. There was the
Cotton-Picking Thread Store – flames
flickering from its roof and the front
windows broken.

And Plog's heart quickened at the
sight of a massive lumpy *thing* just
outside. It was S-shaped,
looking for all the
world like a giant
caterpillar made of
thick red wool and
caked with dust.

Zill stamped on the brakes. "What in the world is that?"

Plog swallowed hard. "This may sound crazy . . . but I think he's some kind of giant sock-monster!"

Chapter Three

SOCKS RUN AMOK

The Squaddies stared at the bright red sock-monster. The 'toe' end was his tail, while his mouth was the hole you would push your foot into.

"He's so big – like a human sock," Furp observed as the thing shuffled inside the store with surprising speed. "Is that what you saw in the fabric factory, Plog?"

"I think so," said Plog. "And now it looks like he's stealing some thread to go with all that material. Come on!"

He threw open the Slime-mobile doors,

and he and his friends charged up to
the shattered shop window. The
stupendous sock was sat inside, sucking
down long strings of cotton like multi-
coloured spaghetti. Suddenly, he swung
round to face them. His black eyes
narrowed – and an almighty blast of
flame belched out from his woolly
throat!

"He's a *killer* sock!" Plog yelled.
"DOWN!"

The Squaddies threw
themselves to the
pavement as the
fireball blazed
over their
heads.

Then
Danjo jumped
up and hurled
himself at the hideous
sock-beast. He banged
and bashed with his pincers
but it was like beating a
cushion; his blows had no effect.

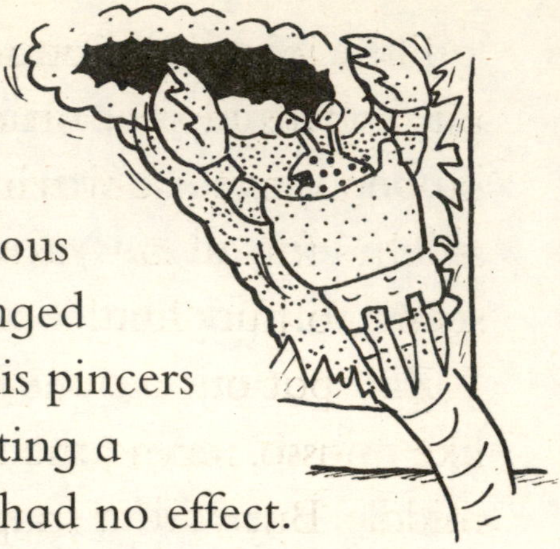

Plog ran to join him, but the sock
swung his head and butted the monster
hard in the chest. "Akk!" He was thrown
through the air and smashed hard
against the wall.

"Fur-boy!" cried Zill,
scrambling into the shop with
Furp. "You all right?"

Plog nodded in
a daze. "Help
Danjo – but be
careful!"

Furp joined the attack on the sock, putting his helmet on his slimy fist like a boxing glove, clobbering the sack of stitches for all he was worth. "Nothing seems to hurt him!"

Zill spat out a slime-line and used it like a lasso, roping the red sock round the middle. But with a snap of his thick neck, he jerked Zill off all six of her feet. "Whoaaa!" She smashed into his lumpy bulk, but managed to hang on, riding him like a human cowboy might ride a runaway bull. The sinister sock reared up and slithered straight towards Plog . . .

"Get out of his way, Fur-boy!" Zill shouted, still clinging onto the sock's back with Furp and Danjo. "We can't control him . . ."

Plog tried weakly to rise – then felt two hands close on his furry shoulders, heaving him out of the way just as the sock smashed clear through the shop front in a hail of bricks and broken glass.

Plog looked up at his unexpected rescuer and got a shock. "Jurley?"

The slim blue monster smiled. "If you can rescue me, I can rescue you back!"

"Thanks," said Plog. "But your factories are way out in Whiffsville – what are you doing here?"

Before Jurley could reply, the bucking
sock came crashing back inside again,
shaking himself furiously. While Zill and
Danjo clung on,
Furp was shaken
free and hurled
against the
wall. Plog ran
over to help
him up – and
found an even
bigger sock
slithering out
from a smoky
back room. He
was sticky and
stripy, and he was chomping down a
dozen reels of coloured cotton.

"Oh, no!" Danjo wailed. "There are
two of those things!"

"Get away, Jurley," Zill shouted at
the factory owner. "It's too dangerous
in here!"

Jurley turned and fled as, with a very rude noise, Stripy raised his 'tail' and fired a sheet of wet, green material at Plog and Furp. They jumped aside and it slapped against the wall, sizzling and steaming.

"Great gonk-stoppers!" Furp cried. "That fabric is covered in poisonous goo. If it had hit us, we would be dead by now."

"Dead!" rasped Red Sock, shaking Zill and Danjo off at last. He stooped and blasted more flames in their direction – the two Squaddies barely hid behind a counter in time.

Stripy turned to Red. "Leave them," he hissed. "We have taken enough thread. There is much more to do."

Red nodded, and with a tangling smash of breaking glass, the killer socks burst through the shop window and into the smoky street outside.

"Come on," said Plog, following them. "We can't let them get away . . ."

"But how do we stop them?" said Danjo.

"You cannot," said Stripy. He pointed his head north and stretched himself out to a near-impossible length – then with a gigantic *BOING!* he pinged away like an elastic band, vanishing over rows of houses into the distance.

"So *that's* how that sock seemed to vanish at the factory," Furp murmured. "Elastic power!"

"Look," Jurley gasped from behind a dustbin. "The red one is stretching too."

"Making himself into a sock-rocket!" Plog grabbed hold of Red Sock's stretchy side. "We can't let him get away as well!"

Furp grabbed the sock's tail. Danjo and Zill jumped onto his woolly back. Even Jurley bravely ran forward and held onto the sock's neck.

"Don't let go," cried Furp. "He can't stretch properly with all of us hanging on."

"I may not be able to *fly*," the sock rumbled, "but I can still travel at speed . . ." And suddenly, the frustrated sock zoomed away down the street, moving like a caterpillar but a thousand times faster, dragging Jurley and the Slime Squad along for the ride.

"Yiiiiiikes!" Plog felt the wind whipping at his ears and the sock slipping through his fingers as

the wriggling beast threw him this way
and that. Zill lost her paw-hold
completely and fell through the air, just
managing to snag the sock's neck with
a slime-line. As Red Sock accelerated
still faster she trailed along behind him
like a six-legged, bushy-tailed kite.

"Can't . . . hold on," Jurley panted.

"You must," Plog urged her. "A fall at
this speed might kill you."

"What about crashing into a wall?"
yelled Danjo, pointing ahead with a
pincer.

Plog gulped. The sock had swung
round a corner and was haring up an
alleyway towards a large brick building.

"Stop!" yelled Zill. "You crazy sock!"

"It's no good," Furp yelled. "We're going to hit!"

"Furp!" Plog shouted as the wall rushed up to meet them. "Grab Jurley and jump out of here. Zill – let go of your slime-line! And, Danjo, make a slime-shield – NOW!"

Furp sprang away with Jurley just in time, skidding across the street on his metal pants. Zill dropped the slime-strand and landed nimbly on a parked van nearby. And Danjo just managed to protect Plog and himself with an umbrella of frozen slime as – KA-THWOOM! – the killer sock charged straight through the wall!

Plog shut his eyes as the brickwork broke apart around him in a storm of stone. He and Danjo were knocked to the floor where the icy shield shattered.

In a daze he saw that they'd smashed through the side of an enormous warehouse full of clothes and boxes. There was an open skylight in the roof – and below it stood not only Stripy, but an even shabbier sock made from stained tartan fabric. Both were rootling about in crates of material. Completely unharmed, Red shuffled over to join them.

Plog watched the socks gravely. "Stripy and his pals must have come here to steal *more* fabric – and since Red couldn't drop in through the roof, he broke in the hard way."

"Look at that manky tartan sock," said Danjo. "Where'd *he* come from?"

"What d'you mean, 'he'?" Tartan retorted crossly. "I'm a girl!" She abandoned the crate and sped towards Plog and Danjo.

Suddenly it was as though the smell of sweaty feet had been turned up to eleven!

"Can't . . . breathe," gasped Danjo. "Too . . . stinky . . ."

His nose and throat burning, Plog stared in horror as the reeking tartan sock-monster loomed over them . . .

Chapter Four

ENTER... CONK-WHOPPER

Furp, Zill and Jurley came running inside to help fight off the socks. But within moments, the terrible smell had sent them gasping to the ground as well.

Through watering eyes, Plog saw Red and Stripy approaching too. "How d'you fight a bad smell?" he muttered. "With an even *worse* smell!" He kicked off his heavy boots just as Red Sock slithered up. The evil woollen warrior hissed

fire at Plog's revolting tootsies, but that
was good — because the faster his feet
dried out, the faster his special brand of
toxic slime would start to flow from his
toes and then . . .

Sure enough, his soles were soon
sticky with stupefying yellow sludge.
A terrible whiff filled the air, and
though the socks had no noses that Plog
could see, they still slithered backwards,
waving about in alarm.

Danjo clutched his
nose. "Good stinking
thinking, Plog."

Zill nodded weakly.
"What sock in the
world would want to go
near feet like yours?"

The three socks were still snarling and
snapping even as they backed away
— but then an extraordinary figure burst
into the warehouse through an inside
door. He was large, pink and tubby,

with a scarlet afro, green robes and a shiny silver sandal on his single ten-toed foot. A gaggle of small blue assistants in lab coats flocked behind him. "What's all this, eh?" the bizarre monster boomed. "Entrance to the Sudz Building is by invitation only!"

"That's Calvin Conk-Whopper," said Jurley, astounded, "the creator of Sudz washing powder. We use it at my factories to wash our fabrics."

Danjo's eyestalks waggled in surprise. "We wash our costumes in Sudz too," he revealed. "Ultra-strong cleaning action with the great smell of old lettuce. Mmmm!"

"Stay back," Plog warned the new arrivals. "You have killer socks in your building."

"Killer socks? Pah!" Conk-Whopper shouted. "More like spies in disguise from a rival washing powder company, trying to pinch my secrets – right, Onzo?"

Onzo, tallest of the small blue assistants and with a brighter white lab coat than the others, nodded keenly. "Right, Mr Conk-Whopper."

Plog shook his head. "I don't think you quite understand—"

"Get your noses out of my giveaway designer clothes," Conk-Whopper bellowed at the killer socks.

Onzo nodded. "Go on, get out of here!"

To Plog's amazement, the socks quickly pointed themselves at the skylight, stretched their elasticated bodies long and tight, and then – *BOING!* – off they zoomed like giant smelly rockets, out of the window in the roof and into the early morning sky. Three distant splashes sounded in the distance.

"At least now we know what PIE detected," said Furp. "Super-elastic sock-monsters whizzing away to wherever they came from."

"From those splashes, they must've landed in the River Mudson," Zill realized. "Now, stick those boots on again, Fur-boy, before my nose falls off!"

"Wait!" Conk-Whopper cried, turning towards his unexpected visitors and the hole in his factory wall. "What is this I see before me? Can it be . . . the Slime Squad?" He hopped over to greet them, his hands pressed together, eyes wide. "Oh, dear dear. What a state!"

"Sorry about your wall, Mr Conk-Whopper," said Plog, pulling on his battered boots. "It's sort of our fault, because—"

"Forget the wall," said Conk-Whopper. "Walls can be rebuilt. It's your costumes I'm worried about. Look at them! You're supposed to be glamorous superheroes and here are your outfits, all filthy and scorched and rumpled.

It won't do, will it, my workforce?"

Onzo and the other blue workers tutted and shook heads and crossed things out on their clipboards.

"Never mind our clothes," said Plog. "We're more worried about those giant killer socks who were just here."

Conk-Whopper chortled. "You're not seriously saying that those socks were dangerous?"

"They've stolen tons of fabric and burned down my factories, Mr Conk-Whopper," said Jurley sadly. "You should watch out. They might try to destroy your place too."

"What?" Conk-Whopper went white, then turned to Onzo. "Check that the Great Sudz Giveaway outfits have not been damaged!"

Onzo and a
swarm of blue
figures rushed
away to obey.

Zill was
intrigued. "Sudz
giveaway outfits?"

"Wow!" Jurley had
crossed over to a box and was pulling
out cool tops and trousers. "These are
amazing. They look familiar . . ."

Conk-Whopper smiled. "You've
probably seen models wearing them on
the catwalks of Goo York," he said
grandly. "These clothes were designed
by top fashion houses like Verscratchy,
Poochi and Blurgerfelt."

"Cool," said Zill. "But giving away
designer clothes must cost a fortune."

"It does," Conk-Whopper agreed.
"But it's fabulous publicity for the
launch of New-formula Sudz
Megawash – the only washing powder

with built-in fabric *toughener*."

Furp cocked his head. "Don't you mean softener?"

"I do not!" Conk-Whopper beamed, slapping an arm round Furp's shoulders. "My fabric toughener makes your clothes far, far stronger. They will never tear or fade or wear out. And New-formula Sudz will work on anything – even metal!"

"Perhaps that's what the socks were after here," said Plog. "As Jurley says, they've stolen masses of material. If they wash it in New-formula Sudz they'll make the fabric tougher . . ."

"And create a whole army of killer socks," said Furp gravely. "An army that will never wear out!"

"The clothes seem fine, Mr Conk-Whopper," called Onzo, scampering back to report. "Nothing's been taken."

"We'd better search this whole factory," Danjo declared. "Just in case there are any other socks here looking for the secret Sudz formula."

"I'll help," said Jurley.

Plog shook his head. "You should go back home. You've been up all night, you must be worn out. Let us handle this."

"But . . . I'd really love to look around the Sudz factory," Jurley persisted.

"Sorry," said Conk-Whopper. "But I cannot let just anyone inside my factory. The secrets of Sudz are worth a fortune." He smiled. "I'm sure you understand?"

"Oh. Er, yes. Of course." Jurley shrugged and waved at the Squaddies. "Well, bye, everyone. Take care, won't you? I've got a feeling you'll be seeing those socks again very soon . . ."

As she turned and walked away, Plog felt a shiver squirm sock-like along his spine. *I've got that feeling too*, he thought. *But whatever those woolly monsters are up to, the Slime Squad will stop them.*

He gulped.

I hope!

Chapter Five

SOCK HUNT

"Now then, my dear Slime Squad," Calvin Conk-Whopper began. "If you are going to come up against these sock-things again, you will need better protection – such as fire-proof, tear-proof clothing."

"He's got a point," Zill admitted.

"Poison-proof and smell-proof would be good too," Danjo added.

"Wear some of my giveaway designer clothes,"

Conk-Whopper insisted. "Pre-washed in New-formula Sudz, they will help shield you from danger."

"Let's test them out," Plog suggested as Conk-Whopper passed him a cool jacket. It looked and felt completely normal – but he couldn't tear a single stitch, no matter how hard he tried. "Danjo, give it a squirt."

Danjo squirted hot slime at the jacket, but it simply splashed sizzling to the floor. "Wow – that's tough."

Zill crossed to a crate and picked out a six-legged trouser suit and strappy top to wear over her grubby leotard. But first she bit savagely at the material. "Cool," she cooed. "Not even a tooth mark."

"Fighting crime and looking *fine*," said Danjo happily, slipping on a checked shirt and three-legged trousers. "I love it!"

Furp started to pull a jumper on over his crash helmet. "You really have something for everyone, Mr Conk-Whopper."

"I'm determined to get the whole of Goo York talking about new formula Sudz," said Conk-Whopper. "Now, I'll give you a guided tour . . ."

"Let's start on the roof," Plog suggested. "The socks used the skylight to get in and out. They might have left a clue up there."

"Right you are." Still followed by Onzo and a gaggle of assistants, Conk-Whopper hopped over to a large lift built into the far wall.

Feeling a bit self-conscious in his smart new clothes, Plog led the Squad over to join him.

The lift lurched into life, taking the group upwards. Conk-Whopper smiled as it clanked to a halt in the cool dawn air. "First stop as requested – the roof!"

Plog marvelled at the incredible view. From here you could see right across Goo York City. The skyline bristled with big, boxy skyscrapers.

Crowds were already forming in the sandy streets below. *Thousands of monsters live here*, thought Plog. *And any of them could be the killer socks' next victim . . .*

"Gracious me," cried Furp, spying a strange assortment of pipes and hoses sticking out from the side of the roof like an extraordinary sculpture. "Whatever's that?"

"Those pipes are attached to a very large tumble dryer a few floors below," Conk-Whopper explained.

Onzo nodded. "We wash and dry hundreds of clothes here every day. The tumble dryer sucks in air, heats it up to dry the clothes, then spits it out through these pipes."

"Very clever," said Furp approvingly.

"And kind of dull." Zill yawned. "No sign of socks up here. Where do we go next?"

"To the Churn-a-rama room!" cried Conk-Whopper, hopping into the lift, his afro a-quiver. "That's where we make New-formula Sudz. Come and see!"

The Squad squeezed in with Conk-Whopper's workers and went down two floors to a large, gleaming metal room. It smelled of mouldy lettuce and was dominated by a massive round paddling pool full of soapy water, churning and bubbling as though seething with nuclear sharks. More employees were working beside the pool, scooping out pails of water and pouring them through sieves to collect a whiffy yellow powder.

"There it is," said Conk-Whopper proudly, leading the way down a steep staircase to the pool. "The powder is dried and put into boxes as New-formula Sudz." He sniffed the air. "Hang on. Something doesn't smell right . . ."

Plog blushed through his fur. "Er, that might be me. When I fought those socks I took my boots off and most of the water spilled out. And when my feet are out of water . . ."

"They go slimy and stink," Danjo put in.

"Yes, I remember." Conk-Whopper smiled. 'Don't worry, my friend. Fill your boots with special Sudz water – you'll make the metal tougher and brighter and your feet will smell great too!"

Plog gratefully took off his heavy boots and filled them with soapy water from the pool. "Ahh," he said as the air smelled only of old lettuce again. "That's better!"

"Too right it is," said Zill cheekily.

"Now then!" Conk-Whopper's cloak rustled as he and his assistants swept up another flight of steps, this time towards a red door. "Next I shall show you the Sudz labs where I invented my amazing washing powder . . ."

The Squaddies followed him outside into a corridor – and Plog heard a distant wailing cry from somewhere at the far end. "Someone's in trouble!" he cried. "Quickly!" He set off at a run with Zill, Furp and Danjo just behind him, cutting a fine dash in their posh new outfits.

"There's nothing that way but the sewing rooms in the basement," Conk-Whopper called after them as his minions milled about in alarm. "That's where the freebie clothes were made ..."

Then Plog skidded to a stop and his friends did the same as the cry was followed by peals of crazy laughter.

Louder and wilder, it echoed up from a spiral staircase at the end of the corridor.

"That sounds like Jurley," Zill realized.

Furp frowned. "But Mr Conk-Whopper said she wasn't allowed to look around."

"She must've sneaked back inside," said Danjo. "But what does she think is so funny?"

"Wait here while I scout around." Plog clenched his fists and ran down the stairs four at a time. But as he burst out at the bottom he couldn't believe his eyes.

There was Jurley, leaning against a door marked 'SEWING ROOM — KEEP OUT'. She was holding a bag stuffed full of half-made designer clothes — clearly stolen from inside. And beside her was a giant killer sock, all ragged and frayed and purple, with nasty yellow spots.

"Jurley!" Plog gasped. "Why were you laughing? What are you doing with . . . that?"

Jurley's eyes were wide as she turned from Plog to the sock. "Get him!" she cried.

And with a room-rocking roar, the spotty death sock obeyed and slithered towards Plog!

Uh-oh, thought Plog. "Look out, everyone!" he yelled up the stairs. "Sock alert!" Even as he spoke, Spotty hurled out a loose thread and lassoed him round the middle. He squeezed and shook Plog hard, this way and that – but thanks to his extra-tough jacket the furry monster could barely feel it. With a hiss of anger,

Spotty threw Plog up the stairs – just as
Danjo and Zill were on their way down.

BAM! Plog struck Zill and she
tumbled into Danjo, who lost his
balance and bumped against the wall.
He aimed a burst of icy-cold slime at
Spotty – but Furp was also bouncing
down the steps and couldn't stop in time.
He thumped into Danjo and knocked
the crab-creature's claw – so the flood of
freezing slime sloshed over Jurley instead!
With a yell she vanished beneath the
chilly blue mess.

"Whoops!" said
Danjo and Furp
together.

"Don't worry,"
Plog panted.
"Jurley's a baddie!
She was stealing
Conk-Whopper's
clothes and she told
the sock to get me."

Furp gasped. "Of course — she's turned up every time we've seen the socks. She must've been working with them all the time!"

"What's happening?" called Conk-Whopper from the top of the stairs.

"There's a killer sock down here!" Plog shouted. "Evacuate the building right now. We'll hold him off."

As Conk-Whopper ran away, Furp leaped forward to fight Spotty. But a loose thread lashed out and caught him round the middle, stopping him in midair. "Good job I'm wearing this extra tough pullover!" he cried as the sock shook and squeezed. "Can't feel a thing!" But then the sock smashed him into the ceiling. Furp yelped as his crash helmet erupted in sparks.

"Furp!" Thinking fast, Zill spat out a slime-line

and tugged him out of the sock's woolly clutches. He smiled at her dizzily, then collapsed.

"You'll pay for that, sock!" Plog yelled.

"No," Spotty gurgled. "YOU will pay for trying to thwart our master's plans . . ." The sock sprinted forward and the cold wet wool of his gaping mouth closed around Plog like a sweaty, stinking vice.

"Hey!" Plog spluttered – as with a disgusting squelching, slobbering noise, the giant killer sock started slurping him up inside!

Chapter Six
SHOCK SOCK CONFESSIONS

"Plog!" Danjo cried, grabbing his friend's legs and trying to pull him back out of the sock's throat.

Zill bit and swiped at the spotty giant. "Give him back, you smelly sack of wool!"

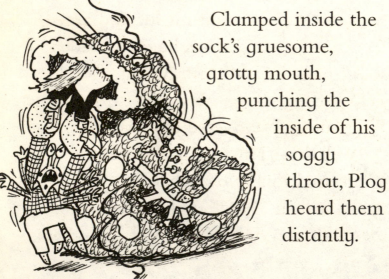

Clamped inside the sock's gruesome, grotty mouth, punching the inside of his soggy throat, Plog heard them distantly.

But every
blow went
BOING! as
it struck the
elasticated
sides. He could
feel himself growing
weaker. If he took a
breath now, the cheesiness might finish
him off.

One last chance, Plog thought. The sock
had sucked him inside up to his bottom
but his legs were still free. He opened
them wide like scissors around the huge
monster, then brought his heavy booted
feet together as hard as he could on the
sock's neck. THWOMP! At last, with a
sick-making slurpy noise, Spotty spat
Plog out and staggered backwards.

"Well done, Fur-boy, you weakened
him," cried Zill. "Now, while he's in a
daze – watch THIS!" Flicking her head,
she spat out a staggering set of slime-lines

that splattered over Spotty, sticking the killer sock fast to the wall.

"And just to make super-sure he stays still," said Danjo, "I'll ice up his little woollen butt!" He fired freezing slime from his cold pincer, icing Spotty silently in place.

"Phew!" Plog wiped his brow. "Well done, everyone."

"We did it," Danjo cheered. "We actually beat one of those things!"

"But not before Spotty beat my crash helmet," said Furp dizzily, studying the dented metal. "I'm OK – but all my gadgets are broken."

"Those socks are tough all right. And Jurley must control them somehow." Plog walked over to the skinny blue monster, still cased in ice and fast asleep on the floor. "She'll just have to make them surrender."

Danjo nodded. "How did she get all the way down to this basement with a giant sock, anyway?"

"I don't know," Plog admitted. Ignoring the KEEP OUT sign, he opened the door to the sewing room. It was dark and shadowy. The floor was piled high with material and patterns. Sewing machines sat on a dozen desks. Plog switched on the light and saw muddy marks on the far wall. "What made those?" he wondered.

"You did it!" Conk-Whopper's familiar booming voice made Plog jump as he came bounding up, his cloak swooshing about him. "You caught a sock – and just as Onzo's sent everyone home for the day."

"Better safe than sorry," said Plog. "We don't know if the other socks are planning to finish whatever they started here." He looked at Furp and sighed. "We'd better tell PIE what happened. He'll tell us what we should do next."

"I'm afraid I can't, my dear Plog." Furp tapped his dented helmet. "My link to PIE is broken. It will take ages to repair it."

"We don't have ages." Plog sighed. "Tell you what – while you stay on guard here, I'll drive back to base in the Slime-mobile and talk to PIE in person. I'll take Jurley with me."

"Good idea," said Zill. "Her socks can't get to her there."

Furp nodded. "And super-smart PIE will soon sort her out."

"Well, I'm glad the rest of you are staying," said Conk-Whopper. "Since I've sent home my workers, perhaps *you* could help stitch the last of my special Sudz giveaway clothes?"

"Do we have to?" grumbled Danjo.

Zill grinned. "I'm afraid *sew!*"

Plog carried sleeping Jurley to the Slime-Mobile. Even wrapped up in an ice-sludge blanket she didn't weigh much. But his heart was heavy. *She seemed so nice and normal*, he thought. *Not like Lord Klukk's usual evil hench-monsters at all . . .*

He drove back to the secret HQ as quickly as he could. Jurley slept all the way, and only stirred a little when Plog entered PIE's office.

71

"WHAT IS THE MEANING OF THIS?" stormed the super-computer.

Plog blinked. "Er . . . meaning of what?"

"Your feet smell of roses!" PIE boomed. "My sensors whiffed it a mile off."

With a cautious sniff, Plog realized PIE was right. The aroma of mouldy lettuce from the Sudz water had changed to something sickly-sweet and fragrant. "Dumb feet," he muttered. "My slime's so toxic, it starts a chemical reaction with just about anything. I've probably turned a harmless washing powder into deadly poison!"

"You have certainly changed it somehow," PIE agreed. "Where are Furp, Danjo and Zill? My sensors saw you fight the killer socks, but then . . . WAIT!" Exclamation marks peppered his computerized face. "You have brought a stranger to our secret base!"

"She's the boss of the socks," Plog explained. "I thought you'd want to question her yourself. Furp's helmet got damaged so we couldn't tell you any other way. He and the others are on guard at the Sudz Building – and Jurley was asleep the whole way so she doesn't know where our base is . . ."

"She must not learn my true identity," PIE hissed. "It is too dangerous." He paused, his sensors pulsing and flickering. "Hang on – Jurley Whirly, owner of the fabric factories that burned down, is the cunning controller of the killer socks? Do you mean to say she wrecked her own businesses?"

"I didn't!" Jurley said weakly, looking up at PIE. "Where am I? What's that?"

Plog remembered what PIE had said about it being dangerous for her to know the computer's true identity. "Um . . . that's my . . . auntie," he said awkwardly. "Auntie PIE."

PIE rattled like he might explode. *"Auntie?"*

Plog cleared his throat. "Er, Jurley, I took you to my aunt's house because she knows a fib when she hears one. So you'd better tell us the truth." He glared at her.

"Like how you just happened to turn up at the Cotton-Picking Thread Store when it was being sock-burgled."

"Coincidence!" Jurley cried. "I was stocking up on new thread, since my whole supply had burned to nothing. I wanted to be served first when they opened. I wasn't expecting another fire – and giant socks ahead of me in the queue!"

Plog snorted. "And what about the way you sneaked into Conk-Whopper's building with a sock?"

"I didn't!" Jurley retorted. "I went inside by myself while you lot were up on the roof, because Conk-Whopper's free clothes were made with fabric stolen from my fabric factories!"

"As if!" Plog scoffed. "Auntie PIE, that's a lie, right?"

"My sensors show she is telling the truth, nephew Plog," said PIE solemnly.

"I only sneaked back so I could find some real proof," Jurley went on. "And I found it in the sewing room. That's why I stuffed my bag full of bits of fabric – I was going to show them to you." She pulled out some samples. "They were *mine* to start off with, see? Moonberry Red and Yellow Snit-Snot – two colours made only by me!"

PIE's screen hummed. "She is telling the truth again – um, Plog dear."

Plog frowned. "But, Jurley, we heard you laughing madly like an evil villain – and you *were* with that spotty sock."

"I laughed madly because he was a *tickling* sock," Jurley explained. "He burst into the sewing room and took me by surprise. He might have tickled me to death if you hadn't shown up."

"But you told him to get me!" cried Plog.

"No, I told you to get *him*!" Jurley shouted back. "And then Danjo iced me up and I banged my head. I wake up here, only to find that you and your  weird-looking auntie think *I'm* behind this whole stinking sock plot – when it's just got to be Conk-Whopper!"

Plog frowned. "Conk-Whopper?"

Jurley nodded fiercely. "He must've used the socks to steal the material for his giveaway clothing – and set the fires to cover his tracks."

"Possibly," said PIE. "And yet every sensor I possess tells me that Lord Klukk is involved in this evil affair. And that means there's a lot more than washing powder and free gifts at stake."

"I think you might be right, er, Auntie." Plog grabbed Jurley's hand and ran from the room. "Come on, we must get back to the others in Goo York and find out what's going on. There's no time to lose!"

Chapter Seven
THE BIG SQUEEZE

"I'm sick of stitching!"
Danjo threw down
his darning needle.
"I shouldn't be in
a sewing room
at all. I'm a
superhero, not a
tailor." He
crossed to the
door and peered
out to check on
Spotty, still slimed
and iced securely in the corridor.
"You know, I was sure that the sock
would've given us more trouble . . ."

"Be grateful," said Zill, her six paws a blur as she sewed the seam of a pretty shirt. "Anyway, we've nearly finished."

"Correction," said Furp. "We *have* finished!" He held up a pair of five-legged trousers and nodded in satisfaction. "There!"

Just then, Calvin Conk-Whopper hopped inside with Onzo. Both wore huge smiles as they saw the big pile of finished clothes.

"Brilliant!" Conk-Whopper boomed, his afro waving as he clapped his several hands together. "And just in time."

Onzo grabbed the clothes and chucked them into a big trolley. "To toughen them up, I'll have them washed in New-formula Sudz straightaway!"

"Thank you." Conk-Whopper smiled as his assistant whizzed out of the room. "Then all we need to do is dry them in the mega-dryer and send them out to the shops, malls and poopermarkets ready for the big launch of New-formula Sudz tomorrow."

"The monsters of Goo York will go crazy for these lovely designer clothes," said Zill. "Everyone will be washing in Sudz!"

Conk-Whopper looked at her. "I certainly hope so. Now, let's follow Onzo to the laundry room!"

The laundry room was on the floor above. It was gigantic! Onzo was already unloading the wet clothes from a turbo-powered washing machine as big as a small house. Furp admired the tumble dryer beside it, which was even larger.

"What a beauty!" Furp declared. "No wonder it needs so many pipes and vents to push all the hot air out into the atmosphere."

"Speaking of heat . . ." Danjo pulled at the collar of his fancy shirt. "Is it just me, or is it getting hotter in here?"

"It's a lot hotter in the dryer!" said Conk-Whopper merrily, hurling open its big round door.

The Squaddies helped shove the Sudz-wet clothes inside. Then Conk-Whopper slammed the door shut and pressed a big red button. With a sound like an exploding rocket, the tumble dryer roared into life — then two seconds later it stopped again.

"Is it broken?" Zill wondered.

"Nope — it's finished!" Conk-Whopper reopened the dryer to reveal a steaming hot pile of clothes inside.

Onzo piled the outfits back into his trolley and wheeled it away. "I'll just take this lot down to the mail room ready for sending," he said.

"I'll give you a hand," said Conk-Whopper kindly. "Back in a minute, Squaddies." As an afterthought, he tossed Furp a stylish broad-brimmed hat. "Here – since your helmet's broken, wear this instead . . ."

Zill and Danjo sat down to wait while Furp popped on his hat and hopped into the dryer for a closer look. "Goodness me, just look at the energy banks in here. This thing can make *far* more heat than you'd ever need to dry off a bundle of clothes . . ."

"You were right about it getting hotter, Danjo." Zill stuck out her tongue, panting softly. "When Conk-Whopper comes back we'll ask him to turn down the central heating."

"And *I* will ask him about this tumble dryer." Furp pushed his head back out, the broad brim of his hat covering his eyes. "It's crazy — its power has been boosted about a million times. You could use it to heat a whole city!"

Danjo pulled again at his collar. "This building's hot enough as it is."

Zill nodded. "And my designer outfit feels very tight all of a sudden."

"Mine too," said Furp. "I think I'll take it off." He tugged at his hat — but it refused to shift. "OW! It's cutting into my forehead."

"This top is squeezing me like a sausage," Zill complained, trying to wriggle out of it. "I can't get it off!"

"My shirt is shrinking!" Danjo stared in horror as the fabric crumpled and cut into his body. "Argh . . . I can hardly breathe, it's so tight."

"Me neither," Furp gasped for air as his jumper crushed against his ribs. "It's almost as though our clothes are attacking us!"

"And the Sudz has made them so tough we can't tear them off," Zill groaned, struggling helplessly on her back. "If they shrink much more they'll squash us to death!"

With a screech of invisible brakes and the smell of burning rubber, Plog brought the Slime-mobile to an emergency stop beside the hole in the wall of the Sudz Building. "Conk-Whopper's got a lot of explaining to do," he told Jurley as they jumped out of the Squad car.

But suddenly, the giant stripy sock they'd met before burst out through the jagged hole in the wall. "BOO!" he rasped, and spat a white blanket at Jurley. It covered her completely and she toppled over.

"It's bound to be poisonous," Plog shouted. "Get it off!" He rushed over to free her – but then Red Sock slithered out of the building and let rip with a blast of flame.

Plog gasped as he felt horrendous heat on his back – then smiled as it quickly faded. "Your fire can't hurt me while I'm wearing this jacket. It's been washed in fabric toughener – the perfect defence!"

"The perfect weapon, more like," Red Sock said smokily, blasting Jurley's blanket with a flaming breath. "That is, once we've heated them up . . ."

"Eh?" Plog felt his jacket growing tighter around his ribs. Red Sock breathed out another two fire blasts – one warmed Plog's front, the other scorched his metal boots. Straightaway, his trousers shrank and squeezed themselves around his furry legs.

His waistband crunched into his tummy. And Jurley was trapped inside her ever-tightening blanket. Only her head was free, and she  stared down in horror as the white fabric pinned her arms to her side and forced her ankles together so she could barely move.

"What's happening?" she shouted.

"The same thing that will happen to anyone who wears clothes washed in New-formula Sudz," Red Sock rasped. "And now you must meet our master . . ."

Plog tried to wriggle away, but Stripy grabbed him in his rough woolly jaws. He saw Red Sock pick up Jurley, then he was swept away by the vicious sock-monster and dragged helplessly into the heart of the building . . .

PTUH! Plog found himself spat out into a very warm room. He landed next to a big tumble dryer – and his heart sank when he saw that his fellow Squaddies had been trussed up by their new togs too.

"Fur-boy!" Zill gasped.

Danjo sighed. "We were kind of hoping you might rescue us."

"Sorry, guys," said Plog as Red Sock spat out Jurley.

"What's *she* doing all trussed up like that?" said Furp, baffled. "Have her socks turned against her?"

"They're not *my* socks," Jurley protested. "They're Conk-Whopper's!"

But the next moment, Tartan slithered inside and spat Conk-Whopper out onto the floor! He gasped and groaned as his shrunken robes squashed his body in some very painful places.

Plog's eyes widened. "Conk-Whopper? But we thought you were in charge!"

Furp tried again. "Have your socks turned against you?"

"They're not my socks," spluttered Conk-Whopper feebly. "They came crashing out of the sewing room downstairs when I was on my way back from the mail room. The red one breathed fire on me and my clothes started shrinking. Lucky I'm not wearing underpants!"

Zill cringed. "Too much information."

"Yeah, never mind your pants," said Danjo. "How come all our clothes have suddenly shrunk?"

"Wouldn't you like to know," came a rasping voice as another nasty sock snuck into the room. It was Spotty, still soggy with melted slime-ice and trailing slime-lines behind him.

With some difficulty Conk-Whopper rolled over to rest beside Plog. "Don't worry," he whispered. "These fiendish socks may have got me, but they didn't get my assistant Onzo. He'll fetch help and get us out of this scrape, you mark my words."

"You are wrong, Conk-Whopper," hissed Spotty. "Onzo did *not* get away . . ."

"Onzo is right here!" The little blue-skinned monster marched into the room, his clothes still fitting perfectly. "You've bossed me around for years, Conk-Whopper, and I'm sick of it! From now on, Lord Klukk and I will boss *you* around. You and every other fool in Goo York City."

"It's *him*," Zill realized with horror. "Onzo is the Lord of the Socks!"

Chapter Eight
STATE OF SOCK

"Onzo?" Conk-
Whopper looked
as though
someone had just
whopped his conk
with a wet fish.
"No wonder the socks
jumped away through the roof when he
told them to leave," Plog recalled. "They
were used to following his orders."

"So now you know – I'm cleverer
than all of you!" Onzo smiled smugly.
"It was *I* who set up Lord Klukk's secret
evil lair next to the sewing room ... *I*
who built an underground entrance to

the sewers for sneaky comings and goings . . . *I* who gave Klukk all Conk-Whopper's material so he could create his sinister sock servants . . . *I* who arranged the fabric factory robberies to *replace* that material so we could make the giveaway clothing . . . *I* who—"

"— is boring us to death," yawned Plog.

"Oh, Onzo." Conk-Whopper shook his head sadly. "I thought you were just working late to impress your boss."

"He was!" came a gruff squawk from somewhere inside Tartan. "*I* am Onzo's *buk-buk*-boss!" Suddenly, the grubby sock coughed up a big lump in her throat – a widescreen smellyvision set that the sock-monster caught in her jaws, displaying the screen to her captive audience.

Plog
saw the
familiar chickeny
silhouette of
Trashland's foulest fowl and
groaned. "Lord Klukk!"

"You're always hiding away," Zill
complained. "You never show yourself."

"And you never learn either," said
Danjo. "Whatever you're planning we're
going to be banning."

"Not this time," snarled Klukk. "Not
now you are prisoners of your own
clothes!"

"I suppose you've made Onzo add
something awful to New-formula
Sudz," said Furp, scrunched up on his

side. "Something that responds to heat, hmm?"

"Correct!" Klukk agreed.

"The clothes are full of pinch-and-pucker particles!" Onzo revealed. "That's *my* name for them!"

"It's rubbish," said Plog.

"I filled the Churn-a-Rama pool with pinch-and-pucker particles," said Onzo. "So they mixed with the washing powder."

Conk-Whopper groaned. "So when the giveaway clothes were washed in Sudz they didn't just absorb my fabric toughener – they absorbed these shrinking particles too!"

"I suppose one burst of heat – like a spin in the jumbo dryer – switches on the particles," said Furp. "Further heat sets them off and causes clothing to shrink!"

Danjo scowled at Onzo. "So it was *you* who turned up the temperature in this building."

Onzo nodded. "We had to test the pinch-and-pucker particles to be certain they worked."

"And now we shall give away deadly clothes to everyone in Goo York," Lord Klukk bragged. "Sudz designer gear will quickly *buk-buk*-become an overnight sensation. Everyone will *buk-buk*-be wearing them and washing their clothes in Sudz. And when everyone is suited and *buk-buk*-booted in pinch-and-pucker particles – the socks shall strike!"

Zill shook her head, baffled. "What good to you is a city full of monsters being strangled by pants and blouses?"

Klukk cackled from the screen. "Goo York is the richest city in Trashland. With most of its population helpless my killer socks will roam the streets, stealing everything of value and crushing anyone who tries to stop them." He puffed up his spiky feathers. "They are the perfect robbers! Their super-elastic *buk-buk*-bodies will let them swallow tons of *buk-buk*-booty and carry it *buk-buk*-back to me.

I'll have enough loot to *buk-buk*-build a thousand more socks and invade all of Trashland . . ."

"But Goo York will be mine," Onzo reminded him. "Once the city has been  plundered, I will step in with the miracle cure for the shrunken clothes." He pulled a test tube from his pocket and waved it around. "I call it 'anti-shrink' – made with puff-and-plumpen particles!"

"That's a worse name than the other one," Plog complained. But his nose twitched at the sweet smell of the antidote. It reminded him of something . . .

"When I single-handedly save Goo York, I shall become a famous hero,"

Onzo said dreamily.
"The grateful public
will beg me to be their
ruler . . ." He stuck out his
tongue at Conk-Whopper.
"Not bad for a poor
assistant from a soap-powder
factory, eh?"

"Oh, Onzo," sighed Conk-Whopper.

"Oh, help!" wailed Jurley.

"Oh, hang on a minute," said Zill.
"This plan is pants. The particles need
strong heat to work, right? Well, you
can't warm up a whole city to get
everyone at the same time, can you?"

"Yes!" Klukk roared with glee. "With
Mr Conk-Whopper's mega-enormous
tumble dryer!"

"Of course." Furp looked helplessly
at his friends. "*That's* why the dryer
has such massive energy banks. It will
generate incredible heat and pump it
out through those pipes in the roof.

The city will get hotter and hotter . . ."

"And my fashion-trap will spring shut!" Klukk broke out into evil laughter. "Face it, you slimy fools – at last, I, Lord Klukk, have *won!*"

Zill, Furp and Danjo hung their heads sadly.

But Plog perked up. Onzo was standing just in front of him, with the tube of anti-shrink poking from his pocket. *I know why I recognize that sickly sweet smell*, he thought. *It's the same smell that's coming from my boots!* "Tell me, Onzo," he said. "How did you make that anti-shrink?"

"It was Lord Klukk who came up with it," said Onzo, bowing quickly to the shadow on the screen. "I believe the main ingredient is some special slime scraped from an old shoebox he found in the Soggy Sewers . . ."

"Shut up, Onzo," Klukk snapped.

Plog's heart thumped harder as his thoughts started to race. *Klukk knows my slime is incredible stuff, and he knows I once lived in the Soggy Sewers. He must've used MY slime to make the anti-shrink!*

"And that means my boot water might do a similar job," Plog muttered. Desperately he tried to catch Zill's eye. At first she frowned. Then she saw Plog nod towards the test tube.

"I get you," Zill said. Quietly she spat out a slime-line and snagged the little tube in Onzo's pocket. With a flick of her head, she yanked it free — and as it smashed on the floor, she flopped on top of it . . .

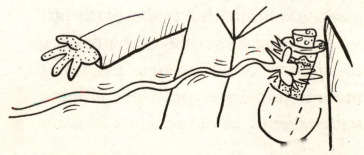

"Yes!" she yelled as Conk-Whopper's clothes loosened up around her. "I can move!" She sprang up into the air and karate-kicked Onzo in the chest.

"Erk!" Onzo warbled, as Zill's power-packed paws propelled him into Tartan at speed. The big sock went down – and so did the smellyvision set clamped in her jaws. Klukk squawked angrily as the screen slammed down on the floor.

Stripy and Spotty swung round to face Zill and lunged forward. But Zill spat another slime-line at the ceiling and pulled herself out of reach, just in time to dodge a jet of flame from Red Sock.

"Stop the poodle-skunk!" raged Klukk.

"You'll have to stop the rest of us too," Plog bellowed. He kicked off one of his boots and it splashed water all over his jacket and trousers.

But nothing happened!

"We shall stop you with ease," hissed Spotty as Stripy, Red and Tartan reared up over the helpless Plog, ready to smack down and squash him into the floor. "Farewell, fool – for ever!"

Chapter Nine

THE PLAN AND THE PERIL

"Come on," Plog muttered, staring helplessly as the boot water spread over his clothes. "You've *got* to work!"

The socks stretched and stiffened, ready for the killer blow . . .

Then, finally – "Yes! My outfit's loosening too!" – Plog rolled aside as the socks came crashing down, and Tartan and Stripy knocked each other flying.

"Nice work, Fur-boy!" Zill pulled off his other boot and splashed the special water inside over Furp. Spotty tried to knock the boot from her paws with a loose thread but the sock-monster was just too slow.

"No!" Klukk screeched. "This is impossible!"

"Not at all!" Furp beamed as the slimy anti-shrink worked its magic on his extra-tight outfit. "You can do such a lot with good quality slime – and Plog's is the best in the business!" As his clothes finally loosened, Furp leaped over a fire blast from Red Sock, grabbed the boot from Zill and emptied the last of the super-water over Danjo.

"Yahoo for the shoe!" Danjo hollered as his own clothes started to unshrink. He jumped aside as Tartan opened her mouth to devour him — then grabbed the dazed Onzo and hurled him down her woolly windpipe instead.

"Stop them, you fools!" Klukk raged as Tartan tried to vomit Onzo back out again.

Plog grabbed Jurley, Danjo picked up Conk-Whopper and everyone charged for the exit. As the Squaddies piled outside, Zill slammed the door shut.

"Furp," said Plog. "If we lure those socks away, can you sneak back inside and destroy Klukk's dryer of doom?"

Furp nodded. "I think so. But it'll take time."

"I can't move much," said Conk-Whopper, "but I'll help all I can."

"Me too," offered Jurley.

"Great." Plog turned to Danjo and Zill. "We have to make the socks chase us away from here."

"Shouldn't be hard." Danjo flinched as the door was nearly thumped off its hinges. "Sounds like they're in a chasing mood!"

Zill helped Furp hide Conk-Whopper and Jurley further down the corridor. Then she galloped back to Plog and Danjo just as the dryer-room door crashed open and a seething bunch of killer socks surged out from inside.

"Run!" roared Plog.

The three Squaddies piled away down the corridor. Red Sock was first after them, belching fire, stretching and shuffling his elasticated body. Stripy was right behind him, Lord Klukk's smellyvision clutched in his mouth so the chicken-thing could watch all the action. Tartan towered above Spotty, who lashed out with loose threads as they raced along – like a woolly lion-tamer cracking a whip.

Furp helped Jurley and Conk-Whopper stagger back into the dryer room – but as they came inside, a sharp shard of concrete bounced off his crash helmet. "Ow!"

"You won't spoil our plans!" It was
Onzo, waving a spring-loaded catapult.
"I'll stop you!"

"Onzo!" Conk-Whopper looked
shocked. "You know very well that
catapults are against company rules."

"Sadly I don't think he's bothered."
Furp dragged Jurley and Conk-
Whopper down behind an upturned
table as more crude concrete missiles
shot around them. "We don't have time
for this," he muttered. "The socks may
return at any moment. If we haven't
demolished that dryer by then, it's
goodbye, Goo York." He shook his
froggy head helplessly. "And if Klukk has
his way, it'll be ta-ta to Trashland too!"

"Whoa!" yelled Zill, swinging round the corner on a slime-line to escape another plume of Red Sock's flame. "These knitted nightmares are too fast to outrun."

"And too strong to fight," Danjo added.

Plog recognized the entrance to the Churn-a-Rama room. "In here," he said. "I have an idea that might slow down the socks a little . . ."

He led his friends inside, pausing at the top of the staircase that led down to the big, circular pool where fresh Sudz was made. "Quick, Zill – spit out a slime-line across the doorway. Make it low."

"Like a tripwire!" said Danjo keenly. "Cool!"

Zill spat out a thin strand of green slime as requested. "How can you trip up a sock?"

Plog gulped as the sounds of boinging and shuffling grew louder. "We're about to find out!"

The door crashed open and the killer socks pushed inside. Sure enough, Red Sock caught himself on the tripwire and overbalanced. The other socks stumbled over him. Danjo, Zill and Plog pushed the struggling socks down the steps with all their might. SPLOOSH! SPLASH! SPLUSH! The evil knitwear fell into the vat of bubbling water. Stripy barely managed to keep the smellyvision set foam-free.

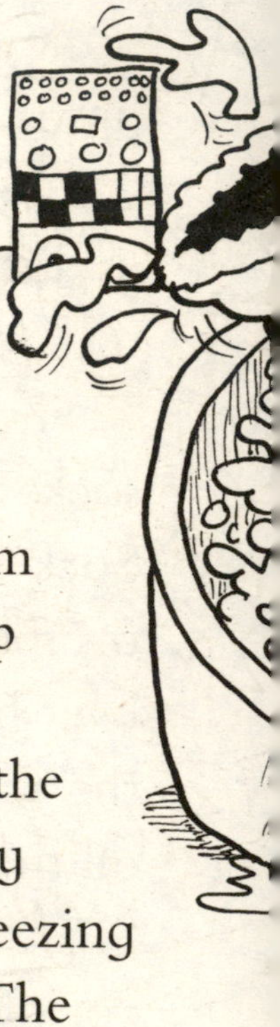

"You
socky chumps!"
Klukk squawked
furiously. "How dare you fall
for such a simple trap!"

"Quickly, Danjo," Plog cried from
the balcony. "Ice up the water. Trap
those things inside!"

"The pleasure is mine, and so is the
slime!" Danjo sprayed plumes of icy
slush down into the pool, swiftly freezing
the water solid. But it was no use. The
sock-monsters swung their bodies from
side to side, cracking open the ice.

Tartan ploughed a path through the half-frozen pool and tore straight through the metal sides of the Sudz vat! Spotty whisked out a thread at Plog – it missed, but sliced clean through the staircase banister.

"Oh, no," Plog groaned. "My plan's backfired. The fabric toughener in the Sudz has made them even stronger."

Zill's tail shot up in the air as the socks surged towards them again. "Run!"

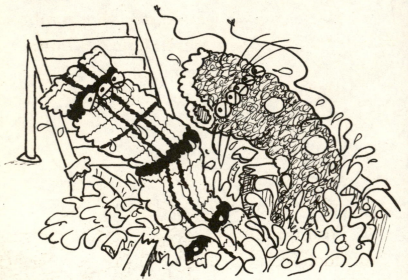

Chapter Ten
IT'S A SOCK-OUT

Back in the dryer room,
Furp was getting more
desperate with every
passing minute. "We
have to stop that jumbo
dryer." He peeped out
from behind the
upturned desk –

and Onzo
nearly shot his
nose off with a
chunk of concrete.
"You need a
distraction,"
Jurley muttered.

"Conk-Whopper, can you kick off your sandal so it flies through the air?"

"Good plan," breathed Conk-Whopper, wriggling onto his back. "Onzo can't fire at my sandal and Furp at the same time . . ."

WHOOSH! Propelled by a flick of Conk-Whopper's toes, the silvery sandal soared upwards.

CRACK! Onzo opened fire.

And at the same moment, Furp pounced out of hiding at incredible speed.

Onzo barely had time to look up before a pair of metal pants collided with his nose! "OUCH!" The overblown assistant collapsed and Furp quickly scooped up

118

his concrete catapult – just as Plog, Danjo and Zill came crashing back inside.

"Those woolly nightmares are right behind us," Zill panted. "Have you wrecked the dryer yet?"

"No!" wailed Furp.

"Good!" Plog replied. "The socks have had a wash in New-formula Sudz. It means they're stronger than ever. But it also means that if we can turn up the heat . . ."

"Of course!" The frog-monster grinned. "One blast of heat will prime the pinch-and-pucker particles, and a second will start them shrinking – just as it did with our own clothes."

Danjo punched the air. "So if we can get them in the tumble dryer, we'll be home and, er, dry – while the socks will be small and shrivelled!"

Zill looked worried. "But how do we get them inside it?"

With a massive crash, the door and the wall around it exploded to reveal the four killer socks in all their savage, slightly soggy splendour.

"Destroy the Slime Squad!" Klukk commanded from his cracked smellyvision set. "Nothing else matters! Nothing!"

Jurley gasped. "*That's* how you have to get them inside – by using yourselves as bait!"

"She's right, it's the only way," said Plog, leading the charge for the dryer. "Come on."

"Wait," Zill gasped as they reached the enormous round door of the machine. "Those Sudzy socks haven't had the first burst of heat yet."

"That's easily fixed," Danjo told her. Hot slime erupted from his left pincer with the force of a firefighter's hose. The socks took a serious dowsing and started to steam. But the bubbling slime only made them even angrier. They slithered towards the Squaddies at breakneck speed, woollen jaws widening . . .

"Tiny flaw in this plan," Zill realized. "If we hide inside the dryer, we'll be trapped – the socks will squish us in seconds!"

"When I checked it out before, I noticed an inspection panel at the back," Furp said breathlessly. "Perhaps we can get through it and double back round."

"It's worth a try," Danjo agreed. "'Cause when danger looms large, the Slime Squad cries—"

"CHARRRRGE!" Plog bellowed. He was the first to fling himself into the cavernous metal drum inside the dryer but the others soon followed. The clatter of Danjo's peg-like feet, Zill's paws and

Furp's pants echoed wildly all around him as the Squaddies ran to a square of metal like a tiny door in the back of the dryer.

Danjo groaned. "*That's* your inspection panel? A flea couldn't fit through that!"

"A flea isn't as tough and determined as we are," Plog told him – as Zill kicked in the panel with four paws and a "Hi-yaaa!"

Red Sock flopped inside the dryer. Spotty threw out a thread and dragged himself inside after his fiery friend as Zill and Furp scuttled through the narrow gap.

Danjo tried to follow them. "Oh, no!"
He waved his legs helplessly. "I'm
stuck!"

Plog glanced behind him and saw
Tartan and Stripy climbing inside, as
Red Sock and Spotty wriggled
relentlessly closer . . .

"Sorry, Danjo," he
said – and kicked
his friend hard up
the bottom!

"OW!" *Pop!*
Danjo was forced
through the hatch.

Dodging a blaze
of sockfire, Plog forced
his way through the small crawl space
and joined his friends. As Zill quickly
spat a web of slime-lines to block the
hatchway, Danjo helped Plog up with a
grin. "Thanks, pal. I've never been so
grateful for a boot up the butt!"

"Come on," Furp urged his friends.

"We've got to get out of here, double round and shut the dryer door on those socks before they know what's happening!"

Exhausted, gasping for breath, the Squaddies ran through a short tunnel of pipe work until they reached a dead end.

"This is the only way out," Furp declared.

Desperate now, Plog, Danjo, Furp and Zill punched, kicked and bit their way through the side of the giant dryer! Free at last, they finally flopped down to the floor.

"Well done," called Conk-Whopper. "Now, close the dryer door, turn the dial to setting two and hit the red button."

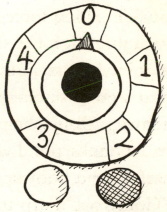

"Quickly!" Jurley added. "The socks are starting to get out again!"

Plog and his friends bundled back round to the front of the tumble dryer. Sure enough, in the big round doorway the socks were already rearing up like horrible serpents. The hunched shadow of Klukk seemed to stare out at them through his two-way screen. "You can never escape, Squaddies!" Klukk gloated. "My socks are indestructible!"

"But that smellyvision set isn't," Plog shouted. He grabbed Furp's broken crash helmet and hurled it with all his strength at the screen. KA-ZTTTT! The set exploded in Stripy's mouth, giving him such a shock that he fell back into his fellow socks, knocking them over.

As the helmet dropped back down to the floor, Zill spat out a slime-line and snagged the dryer door. All four Squaddies heaved on the end to slam the door shut.

Then Furp scaled the side of the towering machine and twisted the main dial. "Setting two, right?"

"Right," said Conk-Whopper. "Two seconds dried a ton of clothes ... so let's see what thirty seconds will do to those evil socks!"

Furp pressed the red button and jumped clear as the machine lurched and shook and rumbled into life,

shaking, tumbling, setting its insides
spinning ever faster . . .

"NOOOOOOOOOO!" Klukk's cries
carried from inside. "I warn you,
Squaddies. The next time we meet it will
buk-buk-be face to face — and a terrible
fate shall *buk-buk*-befall you all!"

"Oh, put a sock in it!" Plog shouted.

The mad chicken-monster's further
ravings were lost beneath the roar of the
dryer as it sent shock waves through the
whole Sudz Building . . .

And then, with a PING! the dryer
stopped. Its door swung open, and four
tiny, shrivelled clumps of wool and fluff
tumbled out from inside.

"So much for the killer socks." Plog
grinned at his friends as they sighed
with relief. "I guess they just couldn't
take the heat!"

Later, once Furp had used Plog's foot
slime and Sudz to whisk up some more

anti-shrink, Jurley and Conk-Whopper were finally free to join the Slime Squad in some post-sock celebrations. They danced and sang and jumped around on the roof – and made plans for the future.

"I'll wash all my free giveaway clothes in anti-shrink and make sure they are harmless," Conk-Whopper declared. "Then the big launch of New-formula Sudz can go ahead safely."

"I'm sure it will be a huge success," said Zill.

Onzo, sitting glumly in the corner, heaved a sigh. "Bah! Not fair!"

"Cheer up, Onzo," Danjo called. "Perhaps they'll use Sudz to wash your prison uniform in monster jail!"

Conk-Whopper turned to Jurley. "I will pay you back, of course, for the fabric the socks stole from you. And all the money Onzo *was* going to get for helping me invent the fabric toughener will cover the costs of rebuilding your factories."

"Thank you," said Jurley. Then she turned to Plog and gave him a hug.

"And thank *you* too. All of you!"

Plog blushed. "Just doing our job, Jurley."

"And doing it with style!" Danjo said happily.

"Now let's go back to base." Zill yawned. "I feel completely washed out."

"Don't mention washing!" groaned Furp.

"It's a shame Klukk got *clean* away," Plog reflected. "But we'll sock it to him the next time we meet – or our name's not THE SLIME SQUAD!"